Written by **Alison Boyle**

Illustrated by **Laura Hambleton**

Milet

How Bees Be

Alison Boyle
Laura Hambleton

Milet Publishing Ltd
6 North End Parade
London W14 OSJ
England
Email info@milet.com
Website www.milet.com

First published by Milet Publishing Ltd in 2003

Text © Alison Boyle 2003
Illustrations © Laura Hambleton 2003
© Milet Publishing Ltd 2003

ISBN 1 84059 332 6

Printed in Singapore

Biker Sis

Bee-rocrats

4

The Nature of Bee-ing
was brought to you by
C. my Bee and Calla my See
A.B.

For the Bees in my Hive:
Parents Jennifer & Brian,
Partner Scott & my best friends
L.H.

Little bee lay in bed, with her honeycomb cover pulled up to her neck.

"Time to get u-u-p," called her sister.

"I can stay here if I like," grumped Little Bee. "I'm a grown-up bee now."

"Places to be, flowers to see!" Biker Sis replied, and she revved her wings and was gone.

Mmmm...breakfast

Little bee lay in bed, with her honeycomb cover pulled up to her chin.

A low hum filled the room.

"Time . . ." urged the softest of voices, "time . . . for breakfast."

"I'll have breakfast when I like," grumped Little Bee. "I'm a grown-up bee now."

"Enjoy your honey while it's sunny," shimmied the breakfast bees, and they revved their wings and were gone.

Little Bee lay firmly in bed, with her honeycomb cover pulled up to her eyes.

A squadron of honeybees whizzed by.

"Time for work!" they chanted.

"I work all day," protested Little Bee. "I ride my bee-bike, I push my bee-buggy, I bake my honey-cakes . . ."

"Nectar to take, honey to make!" the squadron bees chorused, as they revved their hundreds of wings and were gone.

Little Bee was **fuming!**

Honey O's

Honey O's

For a humming start to your day

Little Bee sat up,
got up, went out, turned
right, and revved down
the corridor as fast as
she could.

She screeched to a stop.
A door was blocking
her way. 'Knock Before
Entering' said the sign.

back home

grown-up bees only

Little Bee thrummed
on the door.

"Time to enter!"
came a chirpy voice.

"I'll do what I like,"
snapped Little Bee.
"I'm a grown-up
bee now."

KNOCK
BEFORE ENTERING

Little Bee pushed open
the door and saw . . .

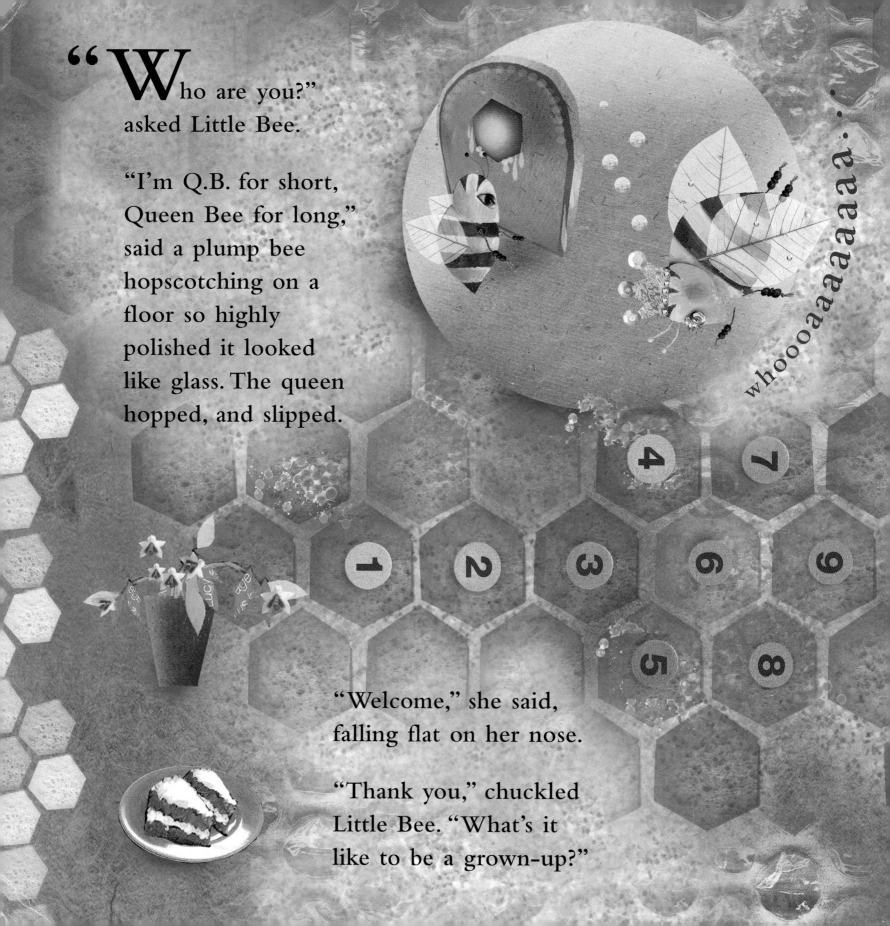

"**W**ho are you?" asked Little Bee.

"I'm Q.B. for short, Queen Bee for long," said a plump bee hopscotching on a floor so highly polished it looked like glass. The queen hopped, and slipped.

whoooaaaaaaaa...

"Welcome," she said, falling flat on her nose.

"Thank you," chuckled Little Bee. "What's it like to be a grown-up?"

"Hmmm, how best to explain?" puzzled Q.B., scratching her double chin with one leg and her royal nose with the other.

"Shall we take a tour?" suggested the queen. Little Bee nodded, and they revved their wings and were gone.

Q.B. and Little Bee

the train tour

in the hot air balloon

After travelling for an hour or two (with Biker Sis following close behind), Q.B. and Little Bee came to a sudden stop.

They stood in front of a whispy door. Q.B. touched it with a flick of an eyelash, and the door disappeared.

in the kitchen

Kitchen Tours

12 o'clock

at the whispy door

ONE WAY

"This," explained Q.B.,
"is where we learn to fly."

6

5

4

"Is it for
grown-ups?"
asked Little Bee.

"Yes," replied
the queen . . .

4:00₀₀

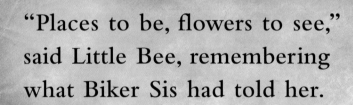

"We must collect pollen from the best flowers, and some are far away."

"Places to be, flowers to see," said Little Bee, remembering what Biker Sis had told her.

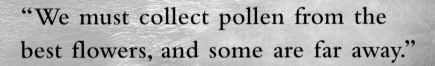

Actually, I'm 1st

On they went, and stopped in front
of a sturdy door. "Uh! Uh!" complained
the queen, struggling to push it open.
Little Bee had to help.

"And this," panted Q.B., "is the bee-rocracy,
where all is kept running smoothly."

"Is it for grown-ups?" asked Little Bee.
"While the sun shines," answered Q.B,
"the flowers blossom and make pollen for
us. We must process it quickly."

"Enjoy your honey while it's sunny,"
remembered Little Bee with a smile.
"Exactly!" said the queen.

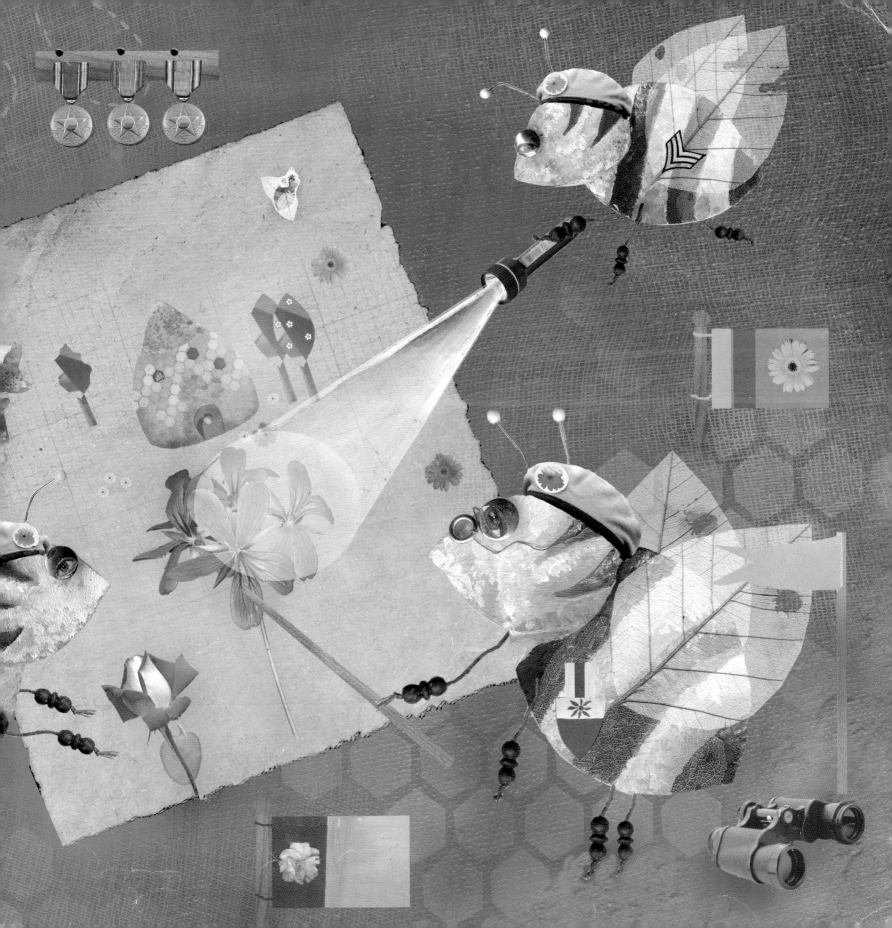

"And here is the factory," announced Q.B. "These noble workers make the honey."

"Is it for grown-ups?" asked Little Bee.

"For everyone," answered Q.B. "The baby bees need lots to eat."

"Nectar to take, honey to make," remembered Little Bee.

The queen bee looked down admiringly at Little Bee. "You are very wise for your age," she said.

"I'm a grown-up bee now," said Little Bee proudly. "Anyway, why don't *you* work?"

The queen was surprised by this question and could not answer it.

"Time" urged Little Bee, in the sweetest of voices, "time for you to start work?"

"Hmmm!" grumped the queen. "I don't see why I should. I'm a grown-up bee now."

Q.B. marched to the next door.

"I know where we are," said Little Bee eagerly, "the dancing school."

"Very good!" praised the queen, happy again. "The dance tells us the way to the flowers with the best nectar."

"Time to dance," sang Little Bee, and she revved her wings . . .

(she was a grown-up bee now, and she could rev her wings when she liked)

. . . and made up
the eight in the . . . .

Sunny
Honey
Dance